"The Happy Pumpkin, Patch"

Written and illustrated by Carol Dabney

"Once again Carol Dabney has written a cute little children's story that has such great qualities. The artwork in this book is so sweet and endearing. All painted by her own hand to match her story. The "Happy Pumpkin, Patch" story reflects a bit of history told in a very easy to grasp way, and has a moral lesson that will help children understand right over wrong." I really enjoyed "The Happy Pumpkin, Patch," simply heartwarming to me. Carol thanks for sharing such sweet stories and art with me and my family, much Aloha -**Arlene Hasegawa** Tutu of the Islands Hilo, Hawaii

What a delight read. A fun book "The Happy Pumpkin, Patch" and learning so much with enchanting illustrations done by author Carol Dabney. –**Linda Nancy** - North East Arkansas Writers Club http://linda-nance.blogsot.com

Patch is a wonderful story about how this country was settled from the view of a pumpkin with a great heart. He was the first pumpkin in the new world. America was a lonely scary place for the first settlers and this story about how a man who had nothing was able to help so many people and meet his new mate through his generosity, by giving away his precious seeds, and making the great pumpkin live forever in the new land. We still celebrate Thanksgiving with lots of pumpkin pie being grateful for all that we have been given, both by the hard working settlers and the wonderful pumpkin, Patch." –**Barbara Funk** Funks Gallery at Etsy.com Shop owner/ Photographer. Pioneer, California

"I loved Patch the pumpkin story. This is not only a book for children, but for all ages. This book covers many worthwhile meanings to life in general. It stresses life, faith, obedience, patience, and then the blessing that comes from these qualities. Beautifully written. I recommend this book to all ages. Carol, thank you for a great book. –**Sandee Teague** Home Health Care/ school nurse, Northeast, Arkansas

"I have known of Carol's work for several years now and she is a very gifted and talented individual. She has been reading and singing with children at schools and composing children's educational songs for many years. She is highly sought after and with her busy schedule READ ALOUD AMERICA and reading at Sgt. Yano Library Schofield Army Barracks and various other schools around the country, I would recommend getting her scheduled as soon as possible. You will not be disappointed!" –**Mike Skelton** Public School Principal Jonesboro, Arkansas

"The one thing that stands out about Carol is her passion within everything she puts her mind to. She does what she does because it is her through-and-through. She believes in her professional projects and her private charities. She has a love of life and doesn't seek the everyday, but seeks the most in each day. Not willing to just go with the flow of normal living, she endeavors to create and to push herself into many experiences to maximize how she can impact the lives of others in a positive way. You can always call her your friend." Respectfully, –**William Cooper,** author /radio personality Eagar, Arizona

This book is dedication to my children
and grandchildren:

Christopher Michael, Ania

John-Joseph, Robin

Melissa Elena,

Jeff, Michelle

Joshua-David Melekamealoha

Noah and Aliyah Melelani

"The Happy Pumpkin, Patch"

www.Amazon.com & CdBaby.Com

https://www.amazon.com/author/dabneycdbooks

The Happy Pumpkin, Patch
book belongs to:

_____

From_____

Date_____

There in the pocket of an
English man, was a tiny seed of an
orange pumpkin.

This pilgrim named Jack
sailed away in a large boat, with
the seed in a locket in his old
worn-out coat.

Together Jack, the locket and
the seed sailed to America
across the wide sea.

Soon the ship arrived at the
great Plymouth Rock.

He was overjoyed as the great
ship docked.

When the time came to pay the captain at the port, the Englishman was sad because he came up short.

For you see he was penniless as he reached in his pocket.

He only had the seed inside the tiny locket.

The sailors all laughed at such a small amount. But the wise old captain gave out a mighty shout.

"One small seed can feed many
for years to come, with tender
care, water and a bit of sun.

Tis better to give than to
receive. Just give to those who
are in need. That would be plenty
pay for me."

That's what the captain said
because he had learned the value
of generosity.

The Englishman was grateful that
the captain was so kind. He
vowed to be faithful and give
back to mankind.

Jack promised to share the seed
so it would multiply. The captain
patted him on the back and
simply answered, "Aye."

In America
the young man would begin a new
life. He'd first plant the seed,
than find a good wife.

Jack dug a hole and placed
the seed in skillfully. He carried
water from the creek and poured
it in carefully.

He prayed each day that it
would be the best. Now time and
the sun would do all the rest.

Finding a good wife was next on his list. He said, "I need someone sweet to hold and to kiss."

He missed his old life and his friends back home, for here in the colonies he felt so alone.

He daydreamed of youngsters to bounce on his knee; and told his dog Daisy, he wanted a large family.

But it seemed that no matter, a
wife couldn't be found. So he
continued to work on his small
plot of ground.

He'd simply have faith in
what he could not see, for a wife
and children, as well as the seed.

Through summer and fall, he'd
just have to wait. Then harvest
time came and he thought it
might be too late.

Sometimes the sun seemed just
a bit too hot,

So Jack took care and watered
his pumpkin seed a lot.

Other times the winds and the storms brought much stress.

The pilgrims could starve if plants failed this test.

But no matter the weather,

he trusted and prayed.

He believed that a miracle

still might come his way.

Then one day a bloom
started to sprout, He was so
happy that he danced all about.

Soon his little seed grew and
grew and grew into the finest
pumpkin anyone ever knew.

Others gathered around to share
in his delight, not taking for
granted this marvelous sight.

The man named his great pumpkin
'Patch,' because after all he'd
grown quite attached.

Now taking the seeds out meant
saying goodbye, and the man he
just couldn't, the thought made
him cry. Cutting into Patch would
bring his life to an end, for
Patch, the pumpkin had become a
good friend.

But Patch assured him,

"I'm feeling quite strong, in fact that's the best way for my life to go on. The seeds inside me should be shared with all others. So go ahead! Pass out the seeds to all of your neighbors."

So the kind man did as he was told. He shared his great gift with the young and the old.

Soon Jack had more friends than he could have ever dreamed. Sharing can often make that happen, it seems.

A sweet maiden watching just
could not resist.

She leaned up to his cheek and
gave him a kiss.

She noticed he was generous and
thought he was fine. For she had
been praying for someone this
kind.

Then she looked at his pumpkin
and the insides were bare. So she
carved out a smile with the greatest
of care.

The man patted the pumpkin and said,
"I've named him Patch." She was
delighted as she lit up a match.

"It's so nice to meet you, goodness where are my manners," then he held out his hand and said, "My name is Jack... Jack O. Lantern."

She giggled as she placed a small light in the pumpkin to shine.

And Patch, the pumpkin felt mighty fine.

Jack fell to his knees, saying
"This is a sign." Then he added,
"Oh please won't you be mine?"

So there was a wedding on that
first Thanksgiving Day.

It's funny how some things just
work out that way.

As the pilgrims gathered with the
Indian nation, Jack held up his cup as
these words were spoken,

"Let us be thankful for this gift of life, our families and friends and now my good wife. The harvest is plenty and we seem to be blessed, with life and love and true happiness."

Patch was delighted, you could tell by
his smile. Soon you could see children
and pumpkins for miles.

The man and his wife gave this gift to
our nation, and that's why to this day
there are pumpkin plantations.

Patch was so happy, he couldn't
be better. For the magic of love
had brought them together.

For there on the ground where
Patch had once laid, the vines
pressed a message that seemed
to say,

"I'm glad I was used to make
such a fine match." Simply signed
from,

"The Happy Pumpkin, Patch."

THE END

My Heart Is Your Home

Wedding song by Carol Dabney

Man, I prayed God would lead me to the one he made for me is you. Feel the beating of my heart, never again to be apart.

Woman, In a gown of soft white lace, I melt in your embrace. Place your ring upon my finger. Vow a love that last forever.

Together, We never have to say goodbye. I'm so happy I could cry. Look at me hear me sigh. We will be together. You never have to be alone. My heart is your home.

Man, You whisper softly in my ear. Create the magic that we share. You're my friend and you're my wife, and I'll give you all my life

Woman, I commit my love to you someone to tell my secrets to, warmed by the glow of the fire, your eyes are pools of desire.

Together, We never have to say goodbye. I'm so happy I could cry. Look at me hear me sigh. We will be together. You never have to be alone. My heart is your home.

Love waits patiently, and gives

endlessly.

My Heart Is Your Home

Composed by Carol Dabney

Sheet Music available separately at

www.amazon.com

Anatomy of a Pumpkin Plant

A pumpkin plant must have water, sun and soil. They have strong roots that grow deep into the ground and soak up water to send up the stem for the plant to drink. The leaves should be green and the bloom of the orange pumpkin is at the top.

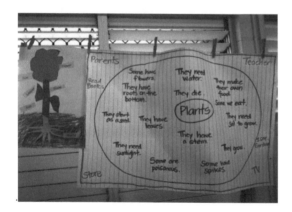

Picture shared from Mrs. Schaefer's classroom at Hale Kula School at Schofield army barracks in Oahu, Hawaii.

How to Plant pumpkins seeds:

Choose an area that gets full sun. Plant the first week in June or when the threat of frost is over. You can plant in a ditch or form a mound of dirt and plant the pumpkin in the center, so the vines have plenty of room to stretch. Plant your seed 2 inches deep. Keep your seed area moist, but don't over water. Your plant should first poke its sprout head out in about 7 days.

Then water well once a week. Water the soil around the plant and try not to get water on the plant or leaves. In about 100 days your pumpkin should have a hard orange shell and be ready to harvest. Make a happy face for Halloween and enjoy your pumpkins.

Roasted pumpkin seeds

Dig out the guts of your pumpkin and you will find the delicious seeds. Preheat oven to 300 degrees. Clean them by using a colander and let them dry thoroughly (even overnight) Mix them in a bowl of melted real butter and sea salt (maybe try garlic salt) Spread the seeds on a baking sheet cookie pan. Bake till golden brown about 45 minutes

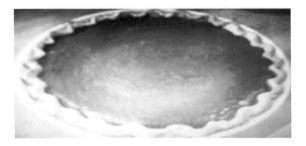

Don't forget to use your pumpkin guts to bake a pumpkin pie or pumpkin bread. Make a Jack-O-Lantern like in the story.

Carol

Dabney: Author, illustrator, composer, recording astist, speaker. Carol has written several children's books: Military Mommy; The Adventures of Noah; 'Twas The Mouse Before Christmas; and her father's biography, Dance Me Home, a true military love story. She was raised on a farm in the Ozarks and studied Italian Opera at the University of Arkansas. She is the mother of five children and has been a music resource teacher, choir director, radio disc jockey, and recording artist. She enjoys traveling and reading at schools around the country.

For readings contact: carol.dabney@yahoo.com

caroldabney@wordpress CDBaby.com ETSY.com

RedWoodsPhotography.com

Dabney books and music available
www.amazon.com & CdBaby.com

https://www.amazon.com/author/dabneycdbooks

The Animals Used By God

Bedtime Bible Series

Write the authors: Martindale & Dabney

902 West Second Street * Little Rock, Arkansas 72201

The Adventures of Noah

Book series about animals, nature and science.

Audiobooks read by the author Carol Dabney

Music composed and arranged by Alwyn Erub

"The Happy Pumpkin, Patch" copyrights 2013

In everything give thanks

Happy Thanksgiving,

From

Carol Dabney

CPSIA information can be obtained
at www.ICGtesting.com
Printed in the USA
LVHW072051281020
670071LV00001B/2